A farmer and his dog went to harvest yams. Suddenly, a yam said, “Get off me!”

The farmer dropped the yam in shock.

"A chatty yam? That's impossible!" cried the farmer.

“It is possible,” said his dog, grinning.

Alarmed, the farmer ran and ran until he got to the market.

He went to tell a fisherman about the chatty yam and dog.

"That's impossible," said the fisherman.

“It is possible,” replied a flapping fish.

In shock, the farmer ran and ran until he got to the mountains.

He went to tell a shepherd about the chatty yam, dog, and fish.

"That's impossible," said the shepherd.

“It is possible,” said a wooly sheep.

Astonished, the farmer ran off to tell the King and Queen.

The farmer ran to tell the King and Queen about the chatty yam, dog, fish, and sheep.

"You foolish farmer," shouted the King. "There cannot be such a thing as a chatty yam."

“Get out and stop telling your silly lies!” ordered the King.

The farmer did as the King requested and left upset.

As the sun set, the King and Queen discussed the farmer and his story about the chatty yam, dog, fish, and sheep.

“Such a silly man,” chuckled the King.

“Yes,” the Queen agreed. “A chatty yam is impossible.”

Suddenly, a wooden stool cried out, “It is possible!”

The King and Queen ran out of the room and off to tell the farmer.